THE
PETER PAN
PICTURE BOOK

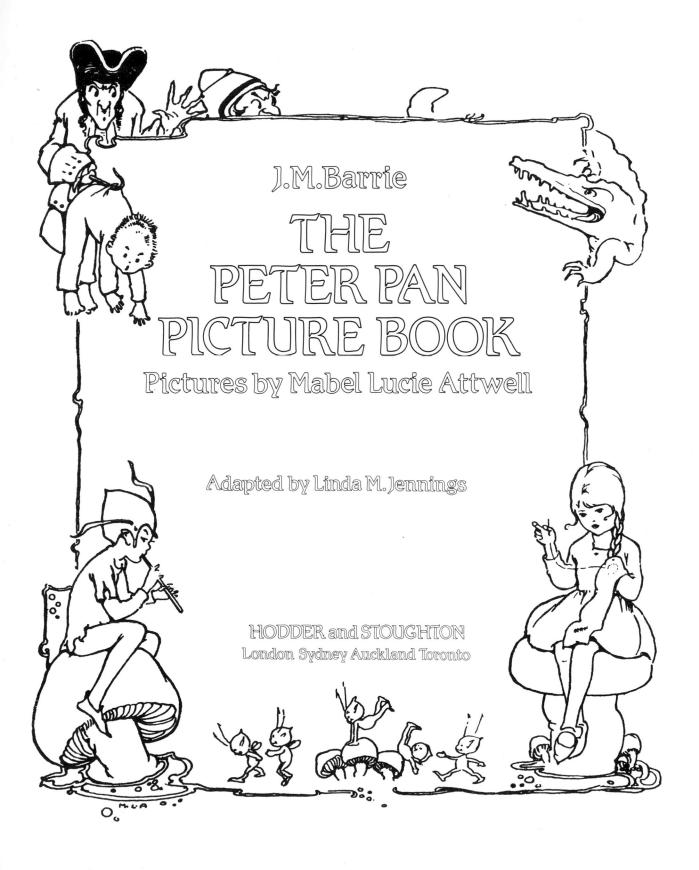

J.M. Barrie
THE PETER PAN PICTURE BOOK

Pictures by Mabel Lucie Attwell

Adapted by Linda M. Jennings

HODDER and STOUGHTON
London Sydney Auckland Toronto

British Library Cataloguing in Publication Data

Jennings, Linda M. (Linda Marion), *1937*
The Peter Pan picture book.
I. Title.　　II. Attwell, Mabel Lucie, 1879-1964
III. Barrie, J. M. (James Matthew, *1860-1937 : Peter Pan)*
823.914

ISBN 0-340-54711-1 hbk
ISBN 0-340-54712-X pbk

This adaptation copyright © Hodder and Stoughton Ltd 1991
Illustrations copyright Lucie Attwell Ltd 1921

First published 1991 by Hodder and Stoughton Children's Books

Published by Hodder and Stoughton Children's Books,
a division of Hodder and Stoughton Ltd,
Mill Road, Dunton Green, Sevenoaks, Kent TN13 2YA

Designed by Trevor Spooner

Printed in Belgium by Proost International Book Production

This is the story of a boy who never grew up, and of the great adventure he shared with Wendy, John and Michael Darling.

The Darling children lived in London with their mother and father. They had a nursemaid too – a big Newfoundland dog called Nana.

Often at night the children would share a make-believe island called Neverland, where a boy called Peter Pan lived. Wendy would sometimes see Peter, sitting at the foot of her bed, playing his pipes.

One night Nana burst into the nursery to find Peter Pan standing on the window-ledge. Nana sprang at the boy and he fled, leaving his shadow behind in Nana's mouth. Mrs Darling found it, put it away in a drawer, and forgot about it. But of course Peter didn't. He wanted his shadow back!

One evening, Mr Darling rather unkindly put Nana out in the yard, and she started barking.

'She smells danger,' said Wendy.

Mrs Darling shivered uneasily, but she kissed the children goodnight before going out for the evening with her husband.

As soon as the parents had left the house, Peter Pan leapt lightly into the nursery. He was not alone. With him was a tiny fairy called Tinker Bell who immediately started to search the wardrobe and drawers.

'It's here, in this big box,' cried Tinker Bell, and Peter Pan pulled out his shadow.

Wendy sat up in bed. She could hear noisy sobs and she found Peter sitting on the floor trying to stick his shadow on with a piece of soap.

'Let me do it,' said Wendy, getting out her sewing-box. 'It may hurt you a little, though.'

'Oh, I shan't cry,' said Peter, and he clenched his teeth as Wendy sewed. As soon as his shadow was attached to him again, he leapt about gleefully.

'How clever I am!' he crowed, quite forgetting that it was Wendy who had helped him.

'Who are you?' asked Wendy, though she knew already.

'I'm Peter Pan.'

'And where do you live?'

'Second to the right,' said Peter, 'and then straight on till morning.'

'What a funny address,' exclaimed Wendy. 'Is that what they put on your mother's letters?'

'I haven't got a mother,' replied Peter. 'I ran away to Kensington Gardens the day I was born and I lived there for a long time among the fairies.'

Suddenly Wendy heard a tiny sound, like bells. 'Is there a fairy in this room?' she asked.

'That's Tinker Bell,' said Peter. He laughed merrily. 'Why, I do believe I've shut her in the drawer.'

And he had! Tinker Bell was furious.

'When I left Kensington Gardens,' Peter went on, 'I went to live with the lost boys. They are the children who fall out of their perambulators, and if they are not claimed, they are sent to Neverland. But we are rather lonely there, for we have no female companionship.'

While Peter was telling Wendy all this, Tinker Bell flew round the room, crying 'Silly ass', 'great ugly girl', and other unpleasant things. She did not like Peter's new friend.

'I heard your mother telling you a lovely story about a lady and a glass slipper,' said Peter.

'That was Cinderella,' said Wendy. 'But I know plenty more stories as well.'

Peter grabbed hold of her and dragged her towards the window. 'Wendy, come with me to Neverland. You could tell us stories, and darn our clothes for us.'

'How can I?' said Wendy. 'I can't fly!'

'I could teach you,' said Peter.

'May John and Michael come too?'

'If you like,' said Peter grudgingly. And when the boys had been woken up Peter took some fairy dust and blew it over them all.

Suddenly they could fly!

It was a long journey, and as they approached Neverland it almost seemed as if something was trying to stop them, but Peter led them safely through.

In Neverland the lost boys, Tootles, Nibs, Slightly, Curly and the Twins, waited for Peter to return. Someone else was also waiting – the villainous Captain Hook, the pirate chief who had an iron hook in place of his left hand. Hook hated Peter, because the boy had chopped off Hook's hand and fed it to a crocodile. Ever since then, the crocodile had followed the captain, because it wanted to enjoy the rest of him! Luckily Captain Hook knew when it was coming, for it had also swallowed a clock which ticked loudly as it went along.

As Peter and the Darling children were approaching the island, something terrible was happening there. Hook's pirate band, who had been following Nibs into the wood, discovered the chimney of the boys' underground home! But it was Peter who the captain wanted, so he noted the spot and, with the pirates, hurried back to the ship, hotly pursued by the ticking crocodile!

Meanwhile, in the sky above Neverland, Wendy became separated from Peter and her two brothers. She found herself alone with Tinker Bell, little knowing that the jealous fairy was planning something wicked . . .

She followed Tinker Bell to the wood where the lost boys lived. Tinker Bell left Wendy hovering in the air, and then she flew down to the boys' underground home.

'Peter wants you to shoot that great white Wendy-bird up there,' she told the boys.

The boys always did as Peter asked, so Tootles took aim with his bow and arrow, and Wendy fluttered down to earth, an arrow in her breast.

'It's not a Wendy-bird, it's a lady!' cried Slightly. 'And you've killed her!'

When Peter returned and saw Wendy lying there as if dead, he ordered the boys to build a little house over her, and he kept guard outside.

'Get out of my sight!' he shouted to Tinker Bell, when he discovered what had happened. 'You are no longer my friend.'

Luckily for Peter and the boys Wendy was not dead. Gradually she recovered and became a mother to them all.

One day, Peter and Wendy were basking on Marooners' Rock, in the middle of a beautiful lagoon, when Peter suddenly sprang to his feet.

'Pirates!' he cried, and he was right, for there in a dinghy were two of Hook's men, with a beautiful Indian princess, Tiger Lily. She was tightly bound hand and foot, and the pirates clearly intended to leave her on the rock till the tide rose.

Peter hid himself, then called out to the pirates in Hook's voice:

'Set her free!'

The two pirates were puzzled at such an order, but they were too afraid not to obey their captain, so they untied Tiger Lily and she swam thankfully away.

When Hook learned of Peter's trick he hurried to the rock to confront the boy. Peter managed to snatch a knife from the captain's belt, but before he could use it, Hook had clawed him with his deadly iron hand.

Tick-tock, tick-tock!

It was the crocodile! The terrified captain leapt from the rock and swam frantically back to his ship.

Too weak to fly off the rock, Peter and Wendy lay side by side, waiting for the tide to cover them or for the mermaids to carry them off.

Just as it seemed as if they would be drowned something light brushed across Peter's face.

It was Michael's kite that had blown away some days beforehand.

'It lifted Michael off the ground,' said Peter. 'Why should it not carry you?'

'Both of us,' said Wendy.

But the kite was not strong enough for them both. Peter tied the tail round Wendy and soon she was lifted off the rock and was blown away out of sight.

Peter was left alone, and the water rose still higher. He tried not to be afraid and a little voice seemed to say to him:

'*To die will be an awfully big adventure.*'

But Peter did not die. Out on the lagoon the Never bird floated on its nest. It had fallen out of a tree once, and had drifted on the water ever since.

'You can float away on my nest,' said the Never bird.

Peter took the bird's two eggs and put them in a hat left on the rock by one of the pirates. Then off he floated on the nest towards home, leaving the Never bird sitting snugly on her hat-nest.

At the very moment Wendy flew down on her kite, Peter too arrived home. All the boys were delighted to see them safe and sound, and the talk of their adventures went on long into the night, till Wendy cried, 'To bed, to bed!' in a voice that had to be obeyed.

The little family in the underground home were very, very happy, for Wendy looked after them like a real mother. The boys thought of Peter as their father, but this worried him, for he did not want to grow up.

Sometimes Wendy would tell the story of how she, Michael and John had flown from the nursery to Neverland.

'Every night Mrs Darling would leave the window open in case they returned,' said Wendy.

'Did they ever go back?' asked Nibs.

'Many years later they did,' replied Wendy. 'And the window was still open.'

'You're wrong!' cried Peter bitterly. 'Mothers aren't like that.' And he told them that his own mother had barred the window against him, and that another child lay sleeping in his bed.

'Oh, let's go home at once, then,' cried Michael.

'Yes,' said Wendy, clutching her two brothers, for she was very frightened by Peter's story.

Peter hated the idea that Wendy meant to leave them, and the lost boys sat gazing at her sadly. Who would look after them now?

'Why don't you come with us?' asked Wendy. 'I could get Father and Mother to adopt you all. You too, Peter.'

But Peter would not go with them, and nothing Wendy could say would make him change his mind.

'Tinker Bell will take you,' said Peter, but before anyone could move there was a terrible noise from above.

Ever since Peter had saved Tiger Lily the Indians had kept a careful watch over the underground home. But now, from the sounds of battle that raged above them, Peter and the others knew that the pirates had made a surprise attack.

It was difficult to tell which way the battle was going – but then, suddenly, all was silent. The only sound was the beat-beat of the tom-toms.

'Who's won?' asked Wendy.

'The Indians, of course,' cried Peter. 'Listen to the drums!'

But he was wrong.

The pirates had chased away the Indians, and had seized their drums. Now they used the drums to trick the children, and sure enough, the boys said goodbye to Peter and came out from the hollow trees, one by one. And one by one they were seized by the pirates and tied up. Lastly, came Wendy. The pirates tied her hands together, and then they flung all the children into Wendy's little house, picked it up, and carried it off to the pirate ship.

Captain Hook stayed behind. His biggest prize lay underground.Quickly he slipped down inside one of the hollow trees to where Peter lay, quite unaware of the danger.

Captain Hook looked down on the impudent, sleeping boy, and he poured a few drops of deadly poison into the medicine cup standing by Peter's bedside.

Then, just as quietly as he had arrived, the wicked captain stole away.

Peter awoke to Tinker Bell knocking at the tree door. As he opened it to the little fairy, he picked up the cup to take his medicine. Tinker Bell immediately snatched it from him and drank the contents herself. The little fairy began to reel about and her bright light dimmed.

'It's poisoned, Peter,' she whispered. 'And now I'll die. I can only live if all the children in the world say they believe in fairies.'

Peter flung his arms out wide and cried to all children everywhere:

'If you believe in fairies, clap your hands – don't let Tinker Bell die!'

Tinker Bell was sinking fast, when she suddenly heard the sound of many children clapping. 'I'm saved!' she said thankfully, and sat up.

Peter now ran all the way to the pirates' ship to help Wendy and the boys. As he swam near, he could see Hook lining up the boys to walk the plank. Wendy had been tied to the mast to watch it all.

'Tick-tock, tick-tock,' went Peter, imitating the crocodile. Captain Hook and his crew were thrown into a panic, and while they were running hither and thither, Peter climbed aboard.

Now there began the most tremendous battle that had ever been seen in Neverland. Peter lured some of the pirates into the cabin, and killed them. He set all the boys free and untied Wendy's bonds. Then, armed with such weapons as they could find, the boys set upon the pirates, who were foolish enough to become separated. Soon every one of them had either been killed or had jumped overboard. The boys closed in on Captain Hook.

'This man is mine,' cried Peter, and he drew his sword. Peter was a superb swordsman, and gradually the captain was pushed nearer and nearer to the edge of the ship, where the crocodile, whose clock had finally stopped, was waiting for him . . .

A final lunge from Peter sent the infamous captain hurtling over the edge into the crocodile's jaws. The battle was won!

Peter knew at last he must say goodbye to Wendy. The children wanted to go home.

'Will you come back each year to help me with the spring-cleaning?' Peter asked her.

Wendy promised that she would.

Back in London Mrs Darling had never given up hope that her children would return to her, and she always left the nursery window open.

Poor Mr Darling felt in his bones that all the blame for their disappearance lay with him for having chained Nana up that fateful evening. He had moved into Nana's kennel, where he vowed to stay till the children returned.

One evening Mrs Darling was sitting in the nursery with Nana's paws resting quietly on her lap. Wendy, John and Michael had been flying through the night towards home, with Peter and Tinker Bell leading the way.

'Go on ahead and bar the window, Tink,' said Peter. 'Then Wendy will have to come back with us again.'

But when he saw Mrs Darling's sad face, he relented and unbarred it again.

'Come on, Tinker Bell,' he cried. 'We don't want any silly mothers,' and off they flew, while Wendy, Michael and John came in through the nursery window.

Mrs Darling thought she was dreaming. But when she touched her children, and realised that they were well and truly home again, she called Mr Darling up from the dog kennel, and there they were, laughing and hugging and kissing, while Peter Pan looked in the window at the happy family scene.

The lost boys waited downstairs till Wendy had explained all about them to her parents, and how they needed a home and a mother. Then up they all came, and Mr Darling looked at them with dismay.

'There are rather a lot of them,' he said.

'We'll fit in, sir,' they assured him, and so it was all settled. Then Wendy opened the window to Peter.

'I would like to adopt him too,' said Mrs Darling, but when Peter learned that he would have to grow up to be a man, he flew off with Tinker Bell to Neverland, where he lived in Wendy's little house that the fairies had put on top of a tree.

For a year or two Peter called for Wendy, and she would go with him to Neverland to help him clean his little house. But then he forgot to come, and Wendy grew up and had her own child.

So Jane, Wendy's daughter, went instead until she, too, grew up, and now it is her daughter, Margaret, who flies away with Peter Pan at spring-cleaning time.